GIA
and the
GIRLS

"A Lesson in Trust"

By Angelo J Peduto

Illustrated by Patrycja Johansen

D1510403

Copyright © 2013 Angelo J Peduto
All rights reserved.
ISBN: 0989454177
ISBN 13: 9780989454179
Library of Congress Control Number: 2013909442
BLUE WAVE

Dedication

To my wife and best friend, Dee Dee,
and my two wonderful children
Gia & Adrian and the "girls" Tres & Delilah.
You all inspire me everyday. I am truly blessed.

Acknowledgement

Thanks to Brad Daberko for his editorial assistance with my first writing venture. A big Thank You to Patrycja Johansen for her wonderful illustrations.

Gia is rudely jolted out of a sound sleep. Her two cats, Tre's and Delilah, or "the girls" as she likes to call them, pounce on her stomach to say "Good Morning". They love to snuggle early in the morning and this exceptionally cold day on Royal Street is the perfect kind of snuggly morning.

"Good morning, girls" says Gia. "I wonder what we can do today?"

The girls nuzzle and prod Gia. They don't want to snuggle this morning... they want to PLAY! Gia knows that Mom will soon pop in to make sure she is getting up and getting ready for the day, but she can never resist the girls.

"Gia!" Mom says in a stern voice. "What are you doing? We talked yesterday about standing on your bed! You told me that I could trust you!"

"I'm sorry, Mommy," Gia replies in her best sorry-pouty voice. "I forgot. I promise that you can trust me to do better tomorrow when the girls wake me up."

Mom smiles and lifts Gia's chin so she can look her in the eyes. "I know you didn't do it on purpose, and I DO trust that tomorrow you will do better. Now, I hope you're hungry... because I made your favorite breakfast – CHEESY EGGS!"

Nothing is better than Mom's cheesy eggs!

"Gia," Mom says "You need to make Tre's and Delilah get down so you can eat your breakfast."

"Girls get down, NOW!" Gia frowns, turns and grabs Delilah, who is behind her, and puts her on the floor. She then makes Tre's jump down from her stool.

"Sorry girls, cheesy eggs are NOT for kitties," she adds and goes back to eating her breakfast.

"Honey?" Mom looks up as she pours Gia some more orange juice. "Do you remember what tonight is?"

"Yeah Mom, how could I forget? It's Daddy's birthday party!" Gia replies.

"Gia, remember we talked about trust this morning?" Mom asks.

"Ummmm... yes...did I do something wrong again?"

Mom smiles. "No, you didn't do anything wrong. I just need your help today and it requires you to be trustworthy. Do you think you can be trustworthy?"

Gia looks up at her Mom. "Of course! Is it something for Daddy's birthday?"

"Yes it is. I need to clean up the basement for the party and I need you to keep Tre's and Delilah out of trouble while I am working." Then Mom looks at her very seriously, "Can I trust you to do that for me?"

Gia's eyes get really big and she jumps up to hug her mom. "Of course Mommy! Anything to help with Daddy's party!"

"This is a great chance for you to prove you're trustworthy... that you will do what you promise to do. Don't let the girls go in the basement while I'm down there."

"I won't."

"And make sure they don't go into the living room or dining room because those rooms are already clean," she adds.

Gia smiles really big and proudly pronounces. "I am trustworthy, Mommy! I will make sure the girls do not bother you or make a mess of the house!"

Mom smiles and kisses Gia on the head.

Gia is now in charge of the girls.

It is very important to Gia that she show her Mom that she can be trustworthy.

"Tres', Delilah, we are going to have so much fun today!" says Gia. "What would you like to play first? OH, I know! We can play like we are going to the park and you two are my babies!"

Gia runs out of the room and comes back with a baby stroller. She puts Tres' & Delilah in the stroller. They are ready to go to the park.

Gia pushes the stroller downstairs. She and the girls are playing in the pretend park when Gia realizes that she has forgotten Anna, her other doll. She dashes back upstairs to get Anna.

But even though she is only gone a short time, it is long enough for the cats to get out of the stroller... and walk into the very clean dining room.

Upstairs, Gia finds her Anna doll, and as she bends to pick it up, she hears a loud CRASH! Gia rushes downstairs to find the cats walking on the table. There is a broken vase and water has spilled all over the special white table cloth. The cats are trying to eat the flowers.

"GIRLS!!! WHAT HAVE YOU DONE?" screams Gia.

Gia crumbles to the floor and buries her face in her hands. Just then Mom walks into the room.

"Gia! What happened?" Mom asks.

Gia looks up with her eyes very red from crying and tries to explain what happened.

"Gia, I know you didn't want this to happen," says Mom. "But did you really think you could trust the girls to stay out of the dining room? Do you think that was the right thing to do?"

"No," Gia says sniffling.

"That's right Gia," Mom continues. "I do trust you. And I also trust that you will learn from this and that next time you will think before you leave the girls alone by themselves."

"I DEFINITELY will, Mom. You're the best Mom in the whole wide world!"

"Thanks Gia. Now let's get this mess cleaned up before the big party!"

"Happy Birthday Daddy!"

THE END

5765982R00016

Made in the USA
San Bernardino, CA
23 November 2013